Contents

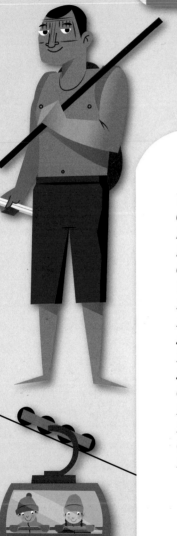

Where is South America?

South America is a triangular-shaped continent that stretches from north of the Equator down towards the Antarctic Circle. Its diverse landscape features rainforests, deserts and glaciers as well as large modern cities and smaller settlements that recall its tribal past.

South America

North America

The Equator runs through the South American countries of Brazil, Colombia, and Ecuador – which is Spanish for 'Equator'.

The border between Panama and Colombia is also the border between the continents of North America and South America.

Caribbean Sea

Panama

Equator

Ecuador

Colombia

Brazil

Locating South America

We can describe the location of South America in relation to the areas of land and water that surround it, as well as using the points on a compass.

- South America is east of the Pacific Ocean
- The Caribbean Sea is northeast of South America
- The Atlantic Ocean is east of South America
- South America is north of Antarctica

Pacific Ocean

Atlantic Ocean

The stretch of water that flows between South America and Antarctica is known as Drake's Passage. It's named after an English sea captain, Sir Francis Drake, who sailed through the area in 1578.

Drake's Passage

Antarctic Circle

Antarctica

Close-up Continents

Mapping South America

Paul Rockett

✳

with artwork by Mark Ruffle

FRANKLIN WATTS

LONDON · SYDNEY

Franklin Watts
First published in Great Britain in 2017 by
The Watts Publishing Group

Copyright © The Watts Publishing
Group 2017

Executive editor: Adrian Cole
Series design and illustration: Mark Ruffle
www.rufflebrothers.com

Picture credits:
Chronicle/Alamy: 10br; Stephanie Colasanti/
Alamy: 8bl; Donatas Dabravolskas/
Shutterstock: 21b; Daniele Falletta/Alamy:
23b; Guentermanaus/Shutterstock: 22bl;
Hakat/Shutterstock: 17br; Robert Harding PL:
27c; Melvyn Longhurst/Corbis: 27tr; Chris
Mattison/Alamy: 13tl; Fernando Quevedo
de Olivera/Alamy: 26; Jurgen Ritterbach/
Alamy:16tl; Edouardo Rivero/Shutterstock:
19br, 25br; Wikimedia Commons: 6-7, 25bl;
World History Archive/Alamy: 10bl.

Dewey number: 918
ISBN: 978 1 4451 4101 5

Printed in China

Franklin Watts
An imprint of Hachette Children's Group
Part of The Watts Publishing Group
Carmelite House
50 Victoria Embankment
London EC4Y 0DZ

An Hachette UK Company.
www.hachette.co.uk

www.franklinwatts.co.uk

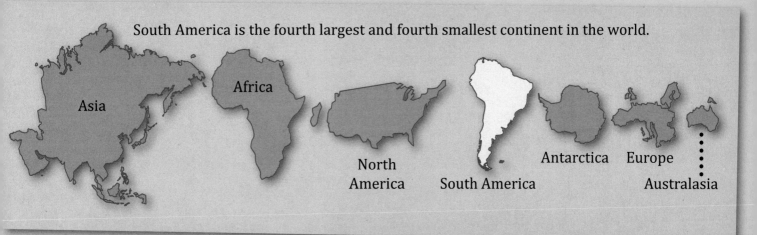

South America is the fourth largest and fourth smallest continent in the world.

Asia

Africa

North America

South America

Antarctica

Europe

Australasia

The Americas

When people talk about 'the Americas' they mean both North and South America. Some geographers define a continent as a single landmass and therefore consider South America and North America to be part of the same continent, known as America. They view South America and North America as subcontinents of America. A subcontinent is an area of land that sticks out separately from the rest of the continent and is surrounded by sea.

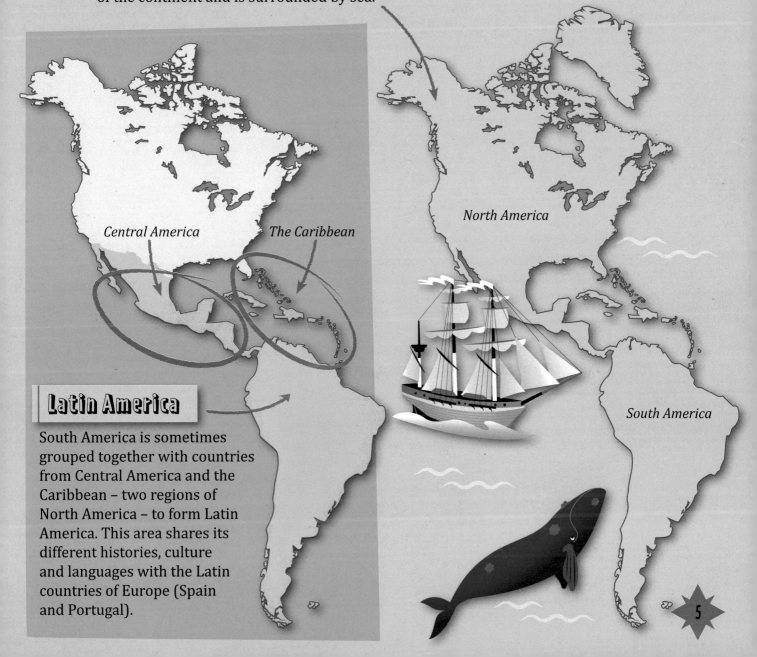

Central America

The Caribbean

North America

South America

Latin America

South America is sometimes grouped together with countries from Central America and the Caribbean – two regions of North America – to form Latin America. This area shares its different histories, culture and languages with the Latin countries of Europe (Spain and Portugal).

5

Countries

South America is made up of 12 countries. It is also home to two small territories that are ruled by European countries: French Guiana, which is part of France, and the Falkland Islands, which are part of the UK.

Brazil is the largest country in South America, measuring 8,515,770 sq km. It is also the fifth largest country in the world.

The smallest country in South America is Suriname, measuring 163,820 sq km. Brazil is almost 52 times its size.

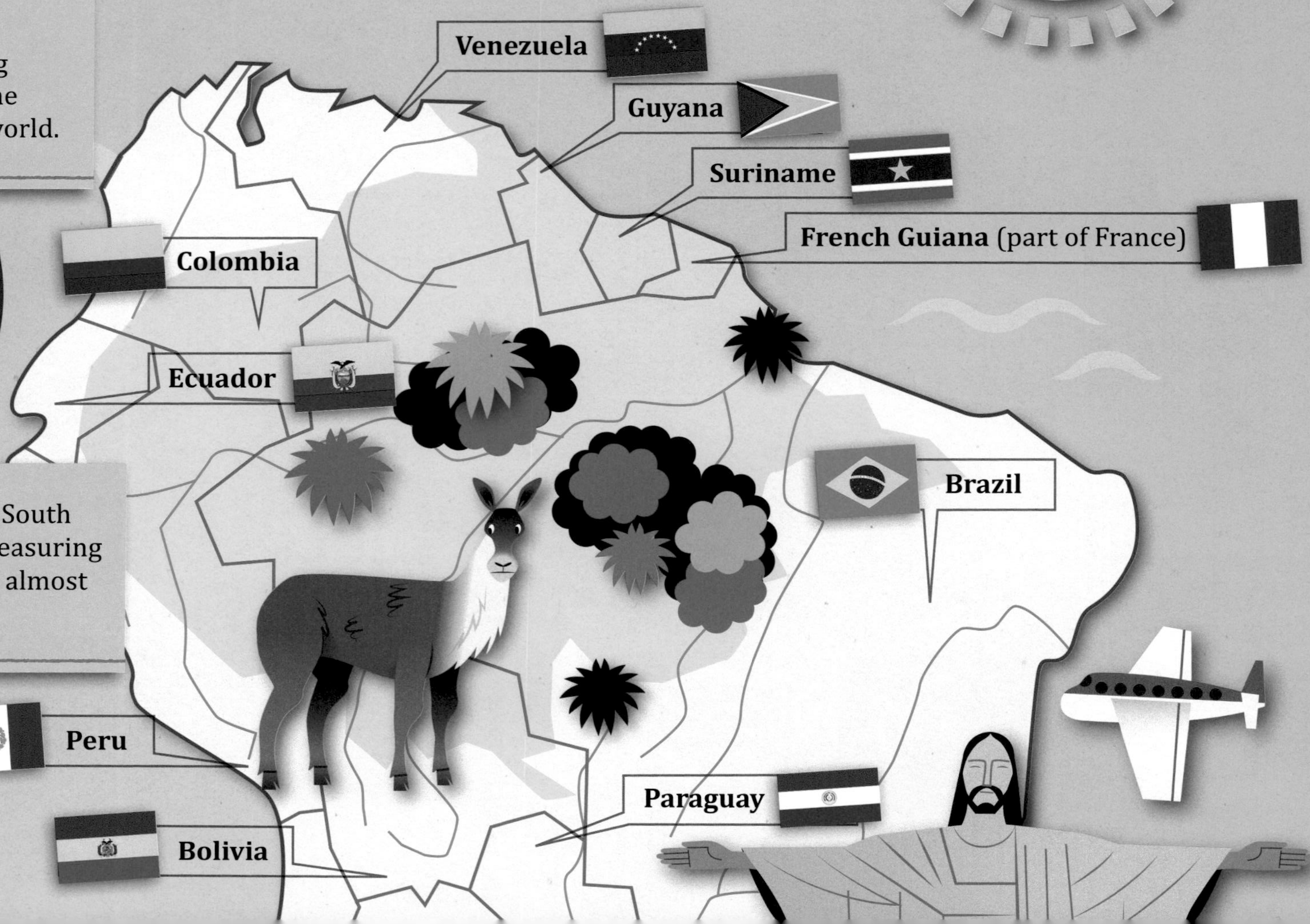

French Guiana (part of France)

Suriname

Guyana

Venezuela

Brazil

Colombia

Ecuador

Paraguay

Peru

Bolivia

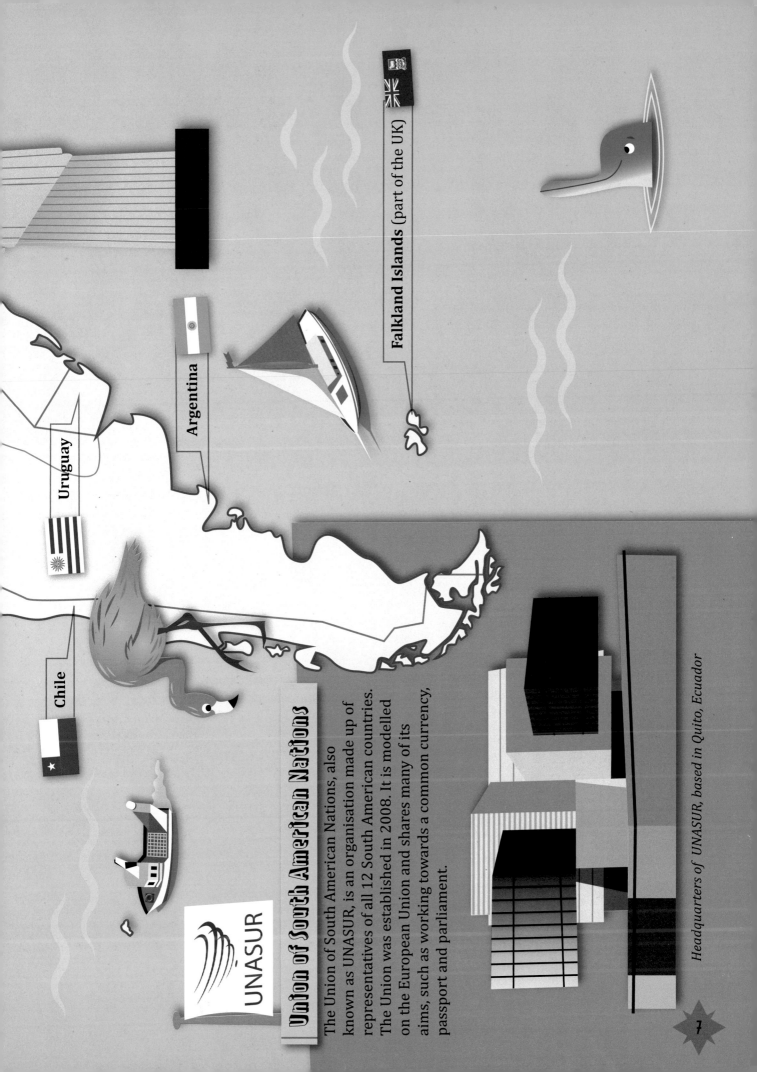

Falkland Islands (part of the UK)

Uruguay

Argentina

Chile

UNASUR

Union of South American Nations

The Union of South American Nations, also known as UNASUR, is an organisation made up of representatives of all 12 South American countries. The Union was established in 2008. It is modelled on the European Union and shares many of its aims, such as working towards a common currency, passport and parliament.

Headquarters of UNASUR, based in Quito, Ecuador

Incas and conquistadors

Humans have been living in South America for over 15,000 years. Many settled in the Andes Mountains. These native inhabitants are called Amerindians and they created a number of civilisations with their own religious ceremonies, agriculture and trade routes. The Incas were the most important of these early civilisations.

= Inca Empire

Paqari-tampu, the original settlement of the Incas

The Incas

The Inca people were originally based in a village called Paqari-tampu in the Andean highlands of Peru. Over a period of less than 100 years, the Incas conquered the territories of neighbouring tribes. By 1525 the Inca Empire was the largest in the whole of the Americas, stretching over 5,000 km from the north of Ecuador down to central Chile.

Golden relic depicting the Inca sun god, found in Peru

ANDES MOUNTAINS

The Incas were skilled architects and road builders, as well as expert farmers and metalworkers. They produced stunning pieces of jewellery and other objects made of gold, silver and precious stones – treasures that entranced European explorers.

Collapsing empire

The arrival of the Spanish in 1532 led to the eventual collapse of the Inca civilisation, although its legacy can be seen in traditional crafts that are still produced today (see page 27).

Conquistadors

European explorers began arriving in South America from the early 16th century. Funded by the kings of Portugal and Spain, they and their soldiers were known as 'conquistadors', meaning conquerors. They made many voyages, exploring different parts of the South American continent.

Christopher Columbus (1451–1506)

Between 1492 and 1496, Italian explorer Christopher Columbus landed on Caribbean islands previously unknown to Europeans. On his third voyage, funded by Spain, he reached mainland South America, landing at the Paria Peninsula in Venezuela on 1 August 1498.

Amerigo Vespucci (1454–1512)

In 1499, Italian explorer Amerigo Vespucci explored the coast of Guyana and Brazil. He went on to map the eastern coast of South America. The 'Americas' is named after him.

Pedro Alvares Cabral (1467–1520)

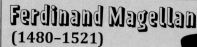

The Portuguese explorer Pedro Alvares Cabral is believed to be the first European to reach Brazil, claiming it for Portugal on 22 April 1500.

Ferdinand Magellan (1480–1521)

Between October and November 1520, Portuguese explorer Ferdinand Magellan was the first European to navigate around the southern tip of South America.

BRAZIL

Pizarro

Francisco Pizarro (c.1475–1541)

On hearing tales of the Incas' riches, Spanish conquistador Francisco Pizarro sailed from Central America to Peru in April 1528. He returned in 1532 and took the Inca emperor, Atahuallpa, hostage, asking for a ransom of enough gold and silver to fill a room. The ransom was paid, but Atahualpa was still executed and Pizarro went on to take control of Peru.

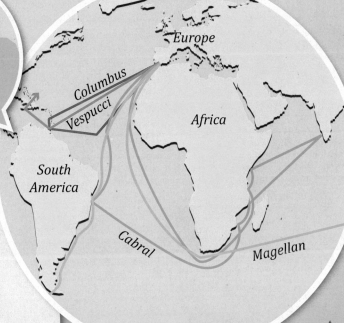

Europe

Columbus

Vespucci

Africa

South America

Cabral

Magellan

Liberation and independence

From the 16th century onwards, Spain, Portugal, the Netherlands, France and Great Britain all set up colonies in South America. They established mines to extract gold and silver, and built large plantations to grow valuable crops, such as sugar. While this created great wealth for the European rulers, it had a devastating effect on the way the South American communities lived their lives.

This map shows the main areas of land controlled by each European country.

Colonial effect

The colonial rulers forced the existing peoples to practise a different religion, speak a new language and to work for them, often as slaves. Europeans also brought over infectious diseases that the indigenous peoples were not immune to, causing thousands to die. As their population dwindled, African slaves were shipped over to work on the plantations and in mines.

Key:

- Spain
- Portugal
- Netherlands
- France
- Great Britain

The image, drawn between 1772–77, shows African slaves arriving in Suriname.

An image from the 1850s shows slaves pounding coffee beans in Suriname.

10

Freedom

Most of the continent was ruled by European countries until the 1800s, when most countries fought for and gained their independence.

This map shows the year in which each country became independent:

VENEZUELA 1811
GUYANA 1966
SURINAME 1975

COLOMBIA 1810

BRAZIL 1822

PERU 1824

ECUADOR 1822

BOLIVIA 1825

PARAGUAY 1811

ARGENTINA 1816

URUGUAY 1825

CHILE 1810

Dom Pedro I
(1798–1834)

Prince Pedro I defied the wishes of the Portuguese government and declared Brazil's independence in 1822. He became known as 'the Liberator' as he supported the Brazilian people in establishing independence, achieving this with little bloodshed and crowning himself as the Emperor of Brazil.

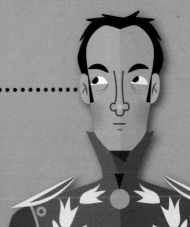

Simón Bolívar
(1783–1830)

Bolívar was a military and political leader from Venezuela. He led revolutions against the Spanish in the north, driving them out of Venezuela, Colombia, Ecuador, Peru and an area referred to as Upper Peru, which was renamed Bolivia in his honour.

Descendants

Today, native South Americans make up just under 45 per cent of the populations of Peru and Bolivia. However, in most South American countries the population is made up of less than 10 per cent of indigenous descendants, with less than 1 per cent remaining in Brazil and Uruguay.

The largest group of people in South America are called *mestizos* – people of mixed European and native South American descent.

Climates

South America's climate is mainly tropical, humid and dry. The tropical weather enriches the rainforest plant life, while the dry weather creates both scorching deserts in the north and colder plains in the south.

Climate Zones:

○ tropical
○ dry
○ humid subtropical
○ Mediterranean
○ marine west coast
○ polar

The wettest place in South America is Quibdo in Colombia, which receives more than 8,900 mm of rain a year.

...The hottest temperature recorded in South America is 48.9°C in the Argentine town of Rivadavia, on 11 December 1905.

Amazon Rainforest

Atacama Desert

Quibdo

Arica

Amazon Rainforest

The Amazon Rainforest remains hot and humid throughout the year. There are two seasons here: a wet season (from December to May) and a dry season (from June to November). Although the wet season rains bring cooler temperatures, it rarely drops below 20°C. While there is less rain during the dry season, conditions inside the rainforest remain wet and humid partly due to the rainforest canopy.

canopy

understorey

The dense leaves of the canopy act as a roof, shielding the understorey from strong sunlight and drying winds. The canopy traps the heat beneath it, along with the moisture that evaporates from the plant life. This keeps the climate hot, wet and humid.

The coldest temperature recorded in South America is -32.8°C in the Argentine town of Sarmiento, on 1 June 1907.

Atacama Desert

The Atacama Desert is thought to be the driest desert in the world – in some parts no rainfall has ever been recorded. On the edge of the desert is the town of Arica which is thought to be the driest inhabited place in the world, even though it is on the coast. It receives on average 0.76 mm of rainfall a year.

The town of Arica, with the Atacama Desert rising up behind it

Tierra del Fuego

Tierra del Fuego is a group of islands divided between Chile and Argentina. The main city here is Ushuaia, the southernmost city in the world. It is also the port from which to sail to the continent of Antarctica.

It is approximately 1,000 km from here to Antarctica, close enough to share elements of its polar climate. Travelling between the two places becomes harder between April and October, when it gets much colder and ice forms, blocking the route.

Ushuaia

Patagonia

Patagonia is a region that covers the southern mainland of Argentina and Chile. It contains areas of vast open spaces, fields of ice, forest and scrubland. The Andes mountain range splits the region, creating a border between the countries of Chile and Argentina, while also affecting the climate on either side.

Patagonia

The wind that blows above the Andes is cold and dry, leaving the Argentine side drier than in Chile, and making the land more arid. The dry area along this side of the Andes is known as a rain shadow.

Westerly wind blows in from the Pacific Ocean bringing with it moisture that falls as rain over Chile.

Andes

Chile

Argentina

Chile

Argentina

Tierra del Fuego

Antarctic Circle

Antarctica

Wildlife

South America is home to more plant and animal species than anywhere else in the world. Here, new species are regularly discovered and, while some animals fight for survival, others have become national emblems.

Pink river dolphin

The pink river dolphin, or boto, is the largest freshwater dolphin in the world. It is found in the Amazon and Orinoco rivers where it feasts on crabs and small fish.

Andean condor

The Andean condor is one of the world's largest birds of prey. It roosts high in the cliffs of the Andes and is the national symbol for many South American countries, including Argentina, Bolivia, and Chile.

Orinoco River
The Llanos
Amazon River
Galápagos Islands
Red-bellied piranha
Amazon Rainforest
The Andes

Isla Santiago
Isla Santa Cruz
Isla Fernandina
Isla San Cristobal
Isla Isobela

Guanaco

The Pampas

Galápagos tortoise

The largest species of tortoise in the world is the Galápagos tortoise. It can grow up to 1.2 m in length and weigh up to 300 kg. It has an average lifespan of 100 years and is only found on the Galápagos Islands (part of Ecuador).

Magellanic penguin

Grasslands

There are two distinct areas of grassland in South America:

The Llanos

The Llanos grassland in the tropical region of Colombia and Venezuela is almost always flooded, attracting reptiles such as the Orinoco crocodile.

The Pampas

The Pampas grassland in Argentina and southern Brazil is drier than the tropical landscape of the Llanos. The climate here makes it perfect grazing land for livestock. Many animals, including the Patagonia mara, live in underground burrows.

Amazon Rainforest

The Amazon Rainforest is the largest area of rainforest in the world. It covers 5.5 million sq km. It's home to millions of species and is estimated to contain one in ten of all the known species on Earth.

Over half of the Amazon Rainforest is located in Brazil, but it also covers areas of Peru, Venezuela, Ecuador, Colombia, Guyana, Bolivia, Suriname and French Guiana.

Discoveries and threats

Scientists are still discovering new species of animals and plants in the rainforest. However many of its known species are at risk of extinction. This is mainly through the destruction of their habitats, with areas of land cleared for large-scale farming and logging. Many animals are also hunted for food and for sport.

Monkeys

There are more than 150 species of monkey in the Amazon Rainforest.

The white-bellied spider monkey is an endangered species. The effects of deforestation and hunting have caused its population to decline by around 50 per cent over the last 50 years.

The Milton's titi monkey was discovered in 2011.

Natural landmarks

The South American landscape ranges from dense tropical rainforest to vast deserts and mountainous highlands. These areas are filled with stunning natural wonders, including large colourful lakes, tall waterfalls and giant glaciers.

Islands in time

The Guiana Highlands cover parts of south-east Venezuela, Guyana, Suriname, French Guiana and the north of Brazil. This is an area of dense vegetation and table-top mountains. The mountains here are sometimes referred to as 'islands in time' as many have remained undisturbed for millions of years.

In 1937, pilot Jimmy Angel crash-landed his plane on top of Auyán-tepui (Devil's Mountain) in Venezuela. Climbing down the mountain, he came across a spectacular waterfall, which thereafter took his name: Angel Falls.

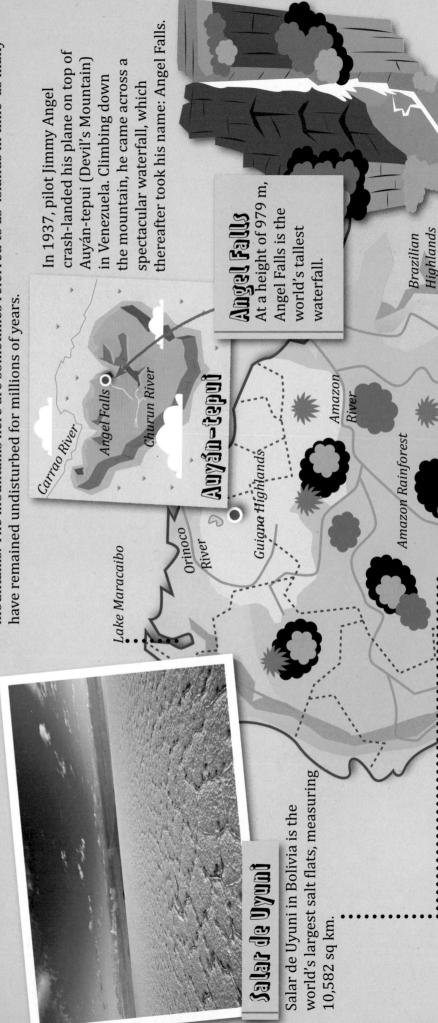

Angel Falls
At a height of 979 m, Angel Falls is the world's tallest waterfall.

Carrao River

Angel Falls

Churun River

Auyán-tepui

Orinoco River

Lake Maracaibo

Guiana Highlands

Amazon River

Amazon Rainforest

Brazilian Highlands

Lake Titicaca

Salar de Uyuni
Salar de Uyuni in Bolivia is the world's largest salt flats, measuring 10,582 sq km.

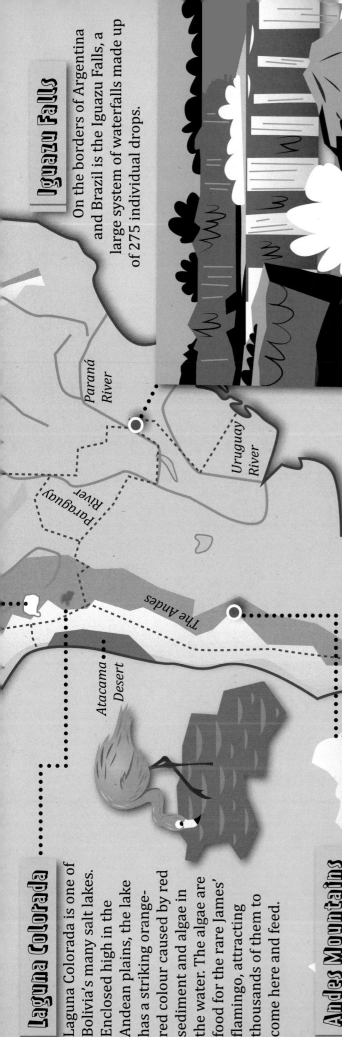

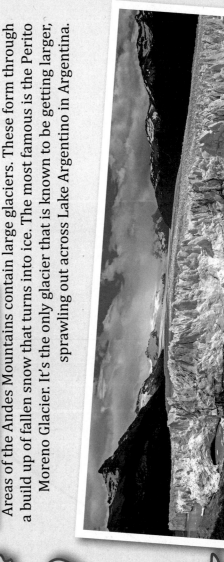

Iguazu Falls

On the borders of Argentina and Brazil is the Iguazu Falls, a large system of waterfalls made up of 275 individual drops.

Perito Moreno Glacier

Areas of the Andes Mountains contain large glaciers. These form through a build up of fallen snow that turns into ice. The most famous is the Perito Moreno Glacier. It's the only glacier that is known to be getting larger, sprawling out across Lake Argentino in Argentina.

Paraná River

Uruguay River

Paraguay River

The Andes

Atacama Desert

Laguna Colorada

Laguna Colorada is one of Bolivia's many salt lakes. Enclosed high in the Andean plains, the lake has a striking orange-red colour caused by red sediment and algae in the water. The algae are food for the rare James' flamingo, attracting thousands of them to come here and feed.

Andes Mountains

The Andes mountain range is the longest in the world and extends through seven South American countries. It forms a natural border between Chile and Argentina, and Chile and Bolivia. The mountains contain many active volcanoes as well as high plateaus with deserts and lakes.

Mount Aconcagua

Mount Aconcagua in Argentina is the highest mountain in South America, measuring 6,960.8 m.

17

Manmade landmarks

Traces of South America's early civilisations can be found in ruined buildings and historic sites. They display advanced skills and ambition, qualities that can also be seen in the continent's modern-day architectural masterpieces.

Machu Picchu

Built in around 1450, Machu Picchu, also known as 'the Lost City of the Incas', is one of the most popular tourist attractions in South America. The city is 2,430 m above sea level and shows the Incas' skill in building around difficult rocky land formations high in the mountains.

The city is divided into different areas, separating the farming area and industrial workshops from the residential areas.

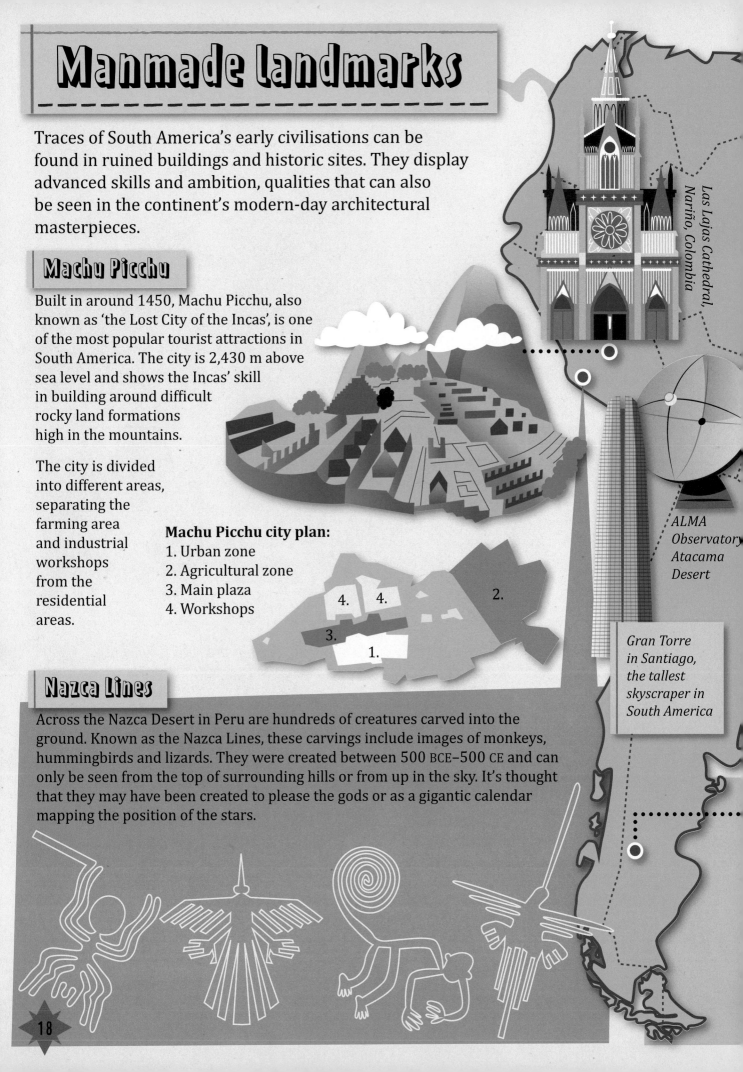

Las Lajas Cathedral, Nariño, Colombia

ALMA Observatory, Atacama Desert

Gran Torre in Santiago, the tallest skyscraper in South America

Machu Picchu city plan:
1. Urban zone
2. Agricultural zone
3. Main plaza
4. Workshops

Nazca Lines

Across the Nazca Desert in Peru are hundreds of creatures carved into the ground. Known as the Nazca Lines, these carvings include images of monkeys, hummingbirds and lizards. They were created between 500 BCE–500 CE and can only be seen from the top of surrounding hills or from up in the sky. It's thought that they may have been created to please the gods or as a gigantic calendar mapping the position of the stars.

Oscar Niemeyer (1907–2012)

Architect

One of the most influential architects of the last century was Brazilian-born Oscar Niemeyer. His buildings are notable for their sweeping curves, giant shapes and use of concrete. He designed many landmark buildings that can be found in Brasília, as well as the United Nations building in New York, USA.

Statue of Christ the Redeemer, Rio de Janeiro, Brazil

Cathedral of Brasília

National Congress Building

Cueva de las Manos

Cueva de las Manos (Cave of the Hands) is in Río Pinturas, the Patagonia region of Argentina. The cave is filled with stencilled outlines of hands and hunting scenes. The images were made between 13,000 and 9,300 years ago.

Settlements

Some of the world's biggest and most populated cities are found in South America, as well as some of the most remote and oldest settlements.

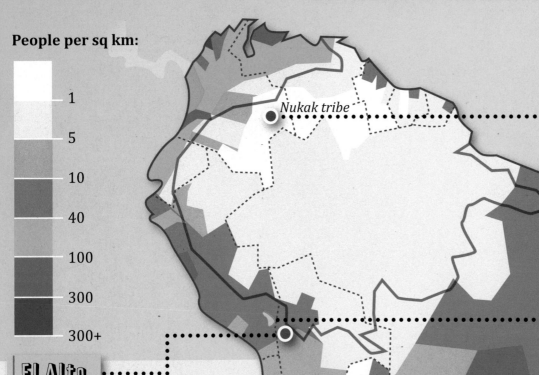

People per sq km:

- 1
- 5
- 10
- 40
- 100
- 300
- 300+

Nukak tribe

El Alto

El Alto is one of Bolivia's fastest growing cities, and one of the highest in the world (El Alto is Spanish for 'the Heights'). It sits on the Altiplano highlands, over 4,000 m above sea level. El Alto enjoys beautiful views along the length of the snow-capped Cordillera Real mountain range, as well as a view of the city of La Paz.

São Paulo

São Paulo in Brazil is home to over 21 million people; it is the largest and most populated city in South America. The city is filled with more than 5,000 skyscrapers, the largest number of high-rise buildings on the continent.

El Alto is connected to La Paz by a cable car system. It was the highest and longest of its kind when it was completed in 2014.

Amazon tribal settlements

There have been human settlements in the Amazon Rainforest for thousands of years, and many tribes still make it their home today. However, their land is not always protected from industrial development and tribes often have to apply for land rights to help ensure that they can continue to live there undisturbed.

The Nukak

The Nukak people are a tribe that live between the Guaviare and Inírida Rivers, near the Amazon basin in Colombia. They roam the rainforest fishing and hunting for food. However, their way of life has come under threat from coca farmers and soldiers that have occupied their land. More than 50 per cent of their tribe have died over the last 30 years, and there are fears that the tribe may soon become extinct.

Floating islands

The Uros people are an indigenous tribe that have been living on floating islands on Lake Titicaca for hundreds of years. There are 42 islands in total, made out of bundled totora reeds that grow in the lake. The islands were first built when neighbouring tribes moved onto the Uros peoples' land. The floating islands allowed the Uros to move about, escaping attacks.

Favelas

Around 6 per cent of Brazil's population lives in shanty towns, also known as favelas. These are poor neighbourhoods with houses made of discarded material, such as cardboard, brick and tin.

The largest favela, Rocinha, is in the Brazilian city, Rio de Janeiro, and is home to over 70,000 people.

Industry

Farming and mining are the biggest industries in South America. More people gain employment from farming than any other industry, while those who work in the continent's large mines extract precious minerals that are in demand all around the world.

Main industries in South America

Crops:
- Bananas
- Citrus fruits
- Corn
- Sugar cane
- Coffee
- Wheat
- Vineyards
- Rubber

Industry:
- Car industry
- Forestry
- Hi-tech
- Textiles
- Fishing
- Tourism

Livestock:
- Cattle
- Sheep
- Pigs

Ecuador is one of the world's largest exporters of bananas.

Bananas

Large-scale farming

In South America, farming generates huge profits for large businesses, with the continent exporting around 10 per cent of the world's food produce. Large areas of land are used for grazing livestock and growing cash crops, such as coffee and pineapple, that can be sold around the world.

The pressure to increase large-scale farming has put much of the Amazon Rainforest at risk. Here, the trees are cut down and replaced with crops or cleared to graze cattle. Crops that are not native to the land, such as soya beans, are planted over large areas leading to soil erosion. Farmers also use pesticides, which impact on the natural wildlife while also harming the long-term use of the land.

Pampas

A rainforest cleared for farming

Beef

Brazil is one of the largest exporters of beef in the world. The production of beef is also important for the economies of Uruguay, Paraguay and Argentina. Large areas of the Pampas (see page 15) are used for cattle ranching, with horsemen, known as gauchos, herding cattle across the grassland plains.

Since the mid-18th century, gauchos have become national symbols for both Argentina and Uruguay.

Mining

As well as mining for energy resources, such as coal and natural gas, South America is also home to a big industry built around mining for precious minerals. Guyana is rich in diamonds and gold, while Paraguay has titanium mines and Colombia produces some of the most sought after emeralds in the world.

Coffee

One of the biggest cash crops in South America is coffee. Almost half of the world's coffee beans are grown here, with Brazil being the world's biggest exporter.

Copper mining

Copper is Chile's largest export, and the country contains over a quarter of the world's copper reserves. Here there are some of the world's largest mines, including the Chuquicamata mine. This is the biggest opencast copper mine in the world, measuring 4.5 km long and 850 m deep.

Small-scale farming

Small-scale farming provides the main source of food for many families living in rural areas, such as villages in the Andes. Known as subsistence farming, people tend small plots of land that produce enough food to feed their family, and sometimes have food leftover to sell.

Sport

Football is the most popular sport in South America, with countries such as Brazil and Uruguay producing some of the world's greatest players. Other major sports include baseball, rugby and beach volleyball, while older tribal games still find keen and competitive players today.

Football

Football first came to South America in the 19th century, when European sailors began playing the game in the port of Buenos Aires in Argentina. Today, all the countries in South America have strong national teams, competing within their own Copa América (America Cup) tournament as well as internationally. While Uruguay's team has won the most Copa América tournaments, the most successful country to compete in the FIFA World Cup is Brazil.

👕 = national team's football shirt

Player profiles

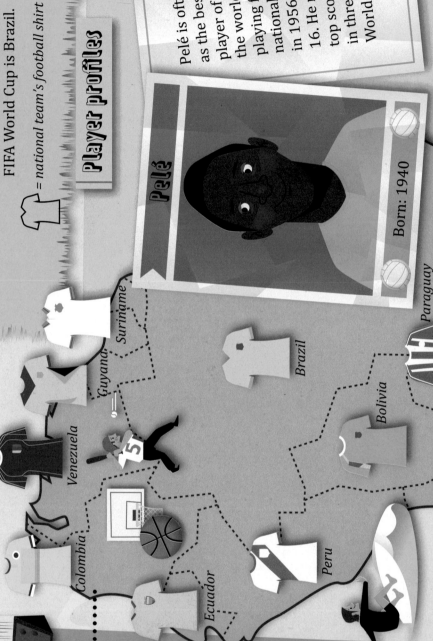

Pelé

Pelé is often regarded as the best football player of all time – in the world. He began playing for Brazil's national football team in 1956, at the age of 16. He remains their top scorer and played in three of Brazil's World Cup victories.

Born: 1940

Guyana
Suriname
Venezuela
Brazil
Colombia
Bolivia
Ecuador
Peru
Paraguay

Tejo

In the Colombian game of tejo, the player has to throw a metal puck at a target 20 m away. The game was originally played over 450 years ago by indigenous tribes who threw objects at a target of gold. The Spanish settlers changed the target to an envelope full of gunpowder – now when the target is hit it explodes creating a big bang!

Women's football is also popular, and Brazilian-born Marta Vieira da Silva is the most celebrated female football player of all time. She has been named FIFA World Player of the Year five consecutive times, and tops the list of Women's World Cup goal scorers.

Marta

Born: 1986

Pato

Pato is the national sport of Argentina. Played on horseback, it traditionally involved two teams throwing around a basket with a live duck inside. The objective was to get the duck-basket to their team's home territory. In the modern-day game, a ball has replaced the duck and basket.

Palín

Palín is one of the oldest sports played in Chile. Similar to hockey, palín is played with long curved sticks used to push along a ball. The Mapuche people played the sport to determine the outcome of tribal disputes.

Uruguay

Argentina

Chile

Culture

While the culture of South America's pre-colonial past is still remembered and celebrated, the continent is also filled with joyful and dramatic music and dance from its more recent history. Religion is also an important influence on the continent's culture, providing the basis for the world's biggest street party.

Carnival

Many Roman Catholic countries have a carnival celebration just before the 40-day period of Lent. During Lent, Catholics are encouraged to fast and live a more austere lifestyle and carnival is an opportunity to enjoy all of the things they'll be giving up. The biggest carnival event in the world is held in Rio de Janeiro in Brazil. Its festivities include five days of parties and dancing, as well as a large colourful samba parade through its streets.

Samba

Samba is a dance as well as a style of music from Brazil that is strongly associated with carnival. Its lively rhythms require dancers to have quick footwork.

Tango

Tango is a type of ballroom dance and music, often performed together. The dance was created towards the end of the 19th century in the slums of Buenos Aires in Argentina. Traditionally, the music is played on a guitar while couples dance close together, striking difficult poses when the music pauses.

Buenos Aires

Inca culture

Although the Inca Empire ended nearly 500 years ago (see page 8), there are communities living in the Andes Mountains that continue to speak their language, practise their crafts and celebrate their music.

Woven textiles made from the wool of alpacas, were highly prized by the Incas. They are still made by Andean people today.

The Siku is a type of panpipe made by the Incas out of reeds. It is still played by the mountain communities of Peru and Bolivia.

The language of the Incas, Quechua, is spoken by around 8 million people in South America today.

Rio de Janeiro

Religion

The largest religion in South America is Roman Catholicism, which was introduced to the continent by the Spanish and Portuguese colonisers. In most countries, over 60 per cent of the population are Roman Catholic; in Argentina the figure is 90 per cent. Two countries that are notably different are Guyana and Suriname, where they have a larger number of Protestants and Hindus. The Protestant faith was brought over by their Dutch colonial rulers, while Hinduism was introduced by immigrants who arrived from India in the 19th century.

The cathedral in Córdoba is the oldest Roman Catholic church in Argentina that is still in use today. Work on the building began in 1598.

Pablo Neruda (1904–1973)

Chilean poet Pablo Neruda was awarded the Nobel Peace Prize for Literature in 1971. He is considered to be one of the greatest poets of the 20th century, as well as an important social and political campaigner. His work ranges from love poems and humorous verses on everyday objects to epic poems about the unfair treatment of people.

Food and drink

Food in South America includes variations on the diets of its indigenous people, as well as influences from Europe. Its large farming industry provides beans, potatoes and fruit, as well as lots of meat.

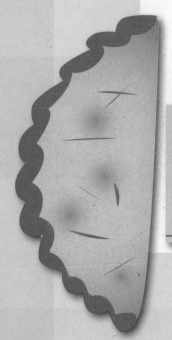

Empanadas

Empanadas are eaten in all South American countries. They are a crescent-shaped pastry usually filled with meat or cheese, which is then fried or baked. The name comes from the Spanish word *empanar*, meaning 'to wrap'. The Portuguese first introduced them into Brazil, and now many different recipes can be found across the continent. Here are some of them.

Brazil

Popular fillings in Brazil include chicken, beef, shrimp and palmito – a vegetable also known as a heart of palm, which is the inner core of certain palm trees.

Ecuador

Empanadas de viento are traditional empanadas from Ecuador filled with cheese, fried and then sprinkled with sugar.

Home of the potato

The potato was originally from South America. The Amerindians farmed it some 1,800 years ago in the Andes region of Peru and Bolivia. It was introduced into Europe in the second half of the 16th century and has since become one of the world's main crops.

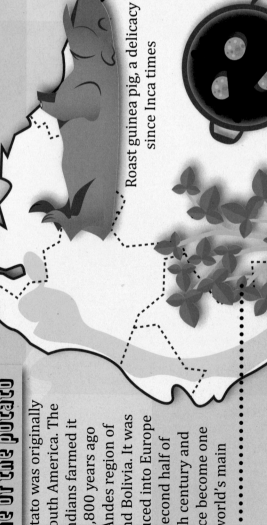

Roast guinea pig, a delicacy since Inca times

Feijoada, a black bean stew

Uruguay

You can also have sweet empanadas; a favourite in Uruguay is made with *dulce de leche*, a caramel sauce made with milk and sugar.

Chile

A traditional Chilean empanada contains a filling called *pino*. This is made of ground beef, onions, raisins, black olives and a hard-boiled egg.

Argentina

Most regions in Argentina have their own traditional filling. In the Salta region of Argentina, they have *empanadas salteñas*, which are small parcels filled with meat, potato, boiled egg and spring onions.

Maté

Maté is a tea-like drink popular in Paraguay, Uruguay, Argentina and Brazil. Made from the dried leaves of an evergreen shrub, it's drunk through a metal straw from a small polished gourd (the hard shell of a fruit). It's thought to have originated from a tribe in Paraguay, and was once believed to hold magic healing powers.

Ceviche

Peru's national dish is *ceviche*. It's made from raw fish marinated in the juice of citrus fruits, served with onions and hot peppers. It's thought that ceviche has been eaten in the coastal communities of Peru for over 2,000 years.

Red wine

Both Argentina and Chile have large vineyards producing world-famous red wines.

Steak with chimichurri

Argentines are big steak eaters and often marinade their meat in a green sauce from the Rio de la Plata region, called *chimichurri*. It's made from finely chopped parsley, garlic, olive oil, oregano and vinegar.

COUNTRY	SIZE SQ KM	POPULATION	CAPITAL CITY	MAIN LANGUAGES
Brazil	8,515,770	204,259,812	Brasília	Portuguese
Colombia	1,138,910	46,736,728	Bogotá	Spanish
Argentina	2,780,400	43,431,886	Buenos Aires	Spanish
Peru	1,285,216	30,444,999	Lima	Spanish, Quechua, Aymara
Venezuela	912,050	29,275,460	Caracas	Spanish
Chile	756,102	17,508,260	Santiago	Spanish
Ecuador	283,561	15,868,396	Quito	Spanish
Bolivia	1,098,581	10,800,882	Sucre/La Paz	Spanish, Quechua, Aymara
Paraguay	406,752	6,783,272	Asunción	Spanish, Guarani
Uruguay	176,215	3,341,893	Montevideo	Spanish
Guyana	214,969	735,222	Georgetown	English
Suriname	163,820	579,633	Paramaribo	Dutch

Glossary

canopy
a dense layer of tree branches that forms a shelter in a rainforest

civilisations
communities that are well-organised with advanced social developments, often forming the basis for later nations

climate
average weather conditions in a particular area

colonies
countries or areas controlled by another country and occupied by settlers from that country

currency
a form of money used in different countries and continents, such as the euro or the US dollar

deforestation
the cutting down and removal of trees in a forested area

dry
a climate zone that receives little rainfall with land that can be too dry to support much vegetation; experienced in areas such as deserts and grassland

empire
a group of countries governed under a single authority, such as under one ruler or country

Equator
an imaginary line drawn around the Earth separating the Northern and Southern hemispheres

glacier
a mass of ice that moves slowly over a large area of land

heritage
items of historical importance for a country, such as buildings, as well as traditions from the past

humid subtropical
a climate zone characterised by hot, humid summers and mild to cool winters

humidity
amount of water vapour in the air

immigrants
people who come to live permanently in a foreign country

immune
to be resistant to a specific disease or infection; immunity can be inherited or administered through medical treatments

indigenous peoples
communities living in a particular country or region that have lived there long before the invasion and settlement of a foreign society, such as the Incas in Peru

Mediterranean
a climate zone with long, hot and dry summers and cool, wet winters

native
born or originating in a particular place, such as people or crops that began life in a certain region

plantation
an area where a specific crop is grown on a large scale

polar
climate zones found surrounding the North and South Poles, which are extremely cold and dry

ransom
an amount of money demanded in payment for the release of someone who has been taken prisoner

textiles
material woven or knitted together, such as cloth

tropical
a climate zone with hot and humid weather and high temperatures throughout the year

understorey
dense layer of plant life, such as shrubs, that grows beneath the canopy of a forest

Index